This book is dedicated to all princes and princesses who will grow to be kings and queens.

I LOVE BEING ME

A short book of positive affirmations for children.

Written By:

Tarjae Greene

Dear little one,
I hope when you read this you find the light within you and realise some of your great qualities. Love being you. You are perfectly and wonderfully made. Never change. You have so much to offer the world. Practice these affirmations to remind yourself so you never forget. Love Tarjae x

I am me,
As me as I can be,
"Come come and see"
Why I LOVE BEING ME.

I am **STRONG**,
as strong as a tree,
as strong as can be,
I love being me.

I am **KIND**,
Helpful and polite,
As kind as can be,
I love being me.

I am **LOVED**,
Loved by many,
As loved as can be,
I love being me.

I am **CONFIDENT**,
I shine like a beam,
As confident as can be,
I love being me.

I am **BLESSED**,
I have a home and food to eat,

As blessed as can be,
I love being me.

I am **BEAUTIFUL**,
Everything about me is unique,
As beautiful as can be,
I love being me.

I am smart,
I can figure out things that are hard,
As smart as can be,
I LOVE BEING ME.

I am **CREATIVE**,
I have lots of amazing ideas,
As creative as can be,
I love being me.

I look in the mirror,
I love what I see,
I am me,
I LOVE BEING ME.

Write down your five new affirmations.

_____

_____

_____

_____

_____

Task

Now practice these affirmations in the mirror every morning by yourself or with an adult!